Ball is published by Picture Window Books,
ne imprint
Crest Drive
ankato, Minnesota 56003
tonepub.com

© 2014 by Picture Window Books

Publication Data is available on the Library
ebsite.
95-2179-1 (library hardcover)
95-3153-0 (paperback)

Ball's class is performing a play based
rite book. Will Krystal get the leading
ortune-telling talents lead her down

Krystal
a Capst
1710 Ro
North M
www.caps

Copyright

Cataloging-in-
of Congress w
ISBN: 978-1-47
ISBN: 978-1-47

Summary: Krysta
on Krystal's favo
role, or will her
the wrong road?

Designer: Kay Fras

Printed in China
092013   00773

Krystal Ball

The GReat and POWeful

by Ruby Ann Phillips
illustrated by Sernur Isik

PICTURE WINDOW BOOKS

Table of Contents

My Future Awaits

Hi there! My name is Krystal Ball. I'm from Queens, which is a part of New York City. Some people call this place the Big Apple. But I live in a tiny, two-bedroom apartment with my mom and dad, so it seems pretty small to me.

Don't get me wrong...I love, LOVE my parents. My mom works as a hair stylist on the first floor of our building. My dad's a high school history teacher. He's always saying things like, "History repeats itself, sweetie." Whatever that means.

I'm not that interested in the past, though. I'm much more excited about...the future.

I like astrology, palm reading, and stargazing. Why? Well, let me tell you a little secret. I'm not exactly normal. I may look small, you see, but I'm really a medium. That means I have a special ability, kind of like a sixth sense. My grandma calls this my "gift." It helps me see what the future holds, but it's never quite clear. I can learn things about a person or an object by touching them and, sometimes, my dreams show little glimpses of events that haven't happened yet.

I usually have trouble understanding these visions, or premonitions, but I'm working on improving my skills. I also go to Nikola Tesla Elementary School, and being a fourth-grade fortune-teller while juggling science projects, math tests, and homework isn't easy.

What else can I tell you about me? Ah! My best friend, Billy, lives in the apartment above ours. I've known him my whole life, and that's a really long time. Almost ten years…Whoa! My other best friend, Claire, is the new girl at school. Both Billy and Claire know about my amazing gift, but they have pinky-sworn to secrecy.

Together, we zip around the neighborhood on our scooters, seeking out adventure. But with my abilities, adventure usually finds us first!

Okay, so you got all that? Good.

Now take a deep breath, relax your eyes, and clear your mind. My future awaits…

CHAPTER 1

Bad Monday

"Oh my stars!" I cried as the school bell rang. I dashed to my seat just as our teacher, Miss Callisto, looked up from her desk.

"Good morning, and happy Monday!" she said, gliding across the floor from her desk to the whiteboard. With a marker, she wrote the day's lesson on the board: DEFINING GRAVITY.

My best friend, Billy, looked at me with a raised eyebrow. "What's up, Krystal?" he asked.

"I would've been here sooner, but I couldn't find my lucky scarf," I said, pointing to the green scarf wrapped around my hair.

"Nice!" said Billy.

"Yeah, SUPER cute, Krystal," joked a voice nearby. It was Emily Heart, the mean girl that sits behind me. "Are you trying to take the attention away from that outfit?"

Okay, so here's the deal...

Normally, I really like school, but recently things have changed. The main reason I wear a scarf on my head is because Emily started to pick on me. She teases me about my bushy hair.

It's totally unfair. So what if she has long, shiny, perfect hair. That doesn't give her the right to pick on me, does it?

Her words stung, and my eyes burned like I was about to cry. I quickly focused on Miss Callisto's lesson. She was talking about Isaac Newton's discovery of gravity.

But I still couldn't concentrate, so I got up to sharpen my pencil. On the way back to my seat, Emily stood and started walking to the pencil sharpener, too. Then *WHAM!* She bumped into me. On purpose!

I felt a surge of bad energy.

The pencil dropped from my hand because of Isaac Newton's gravity. Closing my eyes and tilting my head, I heard it roll across the classroom floor.

A blurry vision formed in my mind. My pencil rolled and rolled and finally stopped at Emily's feet. She picked up her right foot and slammed it down hard on my pencil. The heel of her shoe snapped it in half.

CRAAACK!

The sound sent shivers down my spine.

Suddenly, I heard my name and my eyes snapped open.

It was Miss Callisto. "Krystal, what are you doing out of your seat?" she asked.

"S-s-sorry," I stuttered and sat down quickly. I looked over at Emily, who smiled wickedly.

My cheeks burned. This was not a happy Monday at all. This was a SAD Monday!

* * *

After lunch, we headed outside for recess. I joined Billy and his friends. One of them had a big, bouncy kickball. I could run faster than most boys, so they always asked me to play with them.

It's nice to be popular at something!

As we passed Emily and her friends, Kate and Susan, they each stuck out their tongue. "Looking...sharp!" Emily called out, pretending to write with a pencil.

Billy's friend Joey threw the kickball at their feet. It bounced high over their heads. The girls screamed and scattered.

By the end of recess, I had forgotten all about Emily and her nasty friends. Back inside the classroom, Miss Callisto was waiting for us with a big smile on her face.

"Are you ready for your next assignment?" she asked. "It's an exciting treat for everyone!"

Miss Callisto walked over to her shelf and pulled out a thick book with a gold cover. On the front, the title was written in swirly red type.

I gasped.

"*The Wonderful Wizard of Oz* by L. Frank Baum," Miss Callisto said. "It's my favorite."

That's one of my favorite books, too! I thought.

I couldn't wait to hear what came next. What exciting project would it be? A book report? A scavenger hunt? A diorama? (FYI: I love building dioramas!)

"Our class is putting on a play of *The Wizard of Oz* for the entire school," Miss Callisto announced. "Isn't that, well, WONDERFUL?!"

My dream project quickly became a nightmare! I had no business acting in front of the whole school. I couldn't even stand in front of the class without my knees turning to jelly.

"Here is the script," our teacher said, handing out stacks of stapled paper. "Tonight, I want you to think about which character you'd like to play. We'll be choosing parts tomorrow."

Miss Callisto turned her back to us and began writing our homework on the whiteboard.

"Of course, I'm going to be Dorothy," said Emily to Susan and Kate. "I was born to be a star!" She flipped her hair over her shoulder.

"Weren't you born under a bridge?" Billy asked. "You know, like the other trolls?"

A couple students covered their mouths to keep from laughing out loud.

Emily stuck her tongue out at Billy. "Whatever," she said.

I watched Emily from the corner of my eye. Suddenly, I felt a knot in the pit of my stomach. This Sad Monday was quickly turning into a very Bad Monday.

Would Miss Callisto really give Emily "Evil" Heart the part of Dorothy? I wondered.

I closed my eyes, trying to predict the future, but the voice inside my head replied...

"Cannot predict now."

CHAPTER 2

Welcome to Oz

BRIING!

The bell rang, and the day was finally over. I leaped from my desk and was halfway out the door before the bell even finished.

Billy sprinted to catch up to me. "Wait up, Krystal!" he called out. "What's wrong?"

I told Billy about my vision. Something bad was going to happen to me, and Emily was going to be the cause of it.

I swallowed hard. "Is Emily going to snap me in half like my pencil?" I wondered aloud.

Billy started laughing. "Are you kidding?" he asked. "I could sit on her, and she'd be a street pizza." Then his mind drifted off to his favorite subject. "Mmm...pizza," he said dreamily. "Let's go. I'm starving!"

When we reached the edge of the schoolyard, I spotted my mom. I was so relieved. Without a word, I ran into her arms and hugged her tight.

"Oh!" Mom said, startled by my greeting. "Hello, honey. How are you?"

"Mmmfffff," I said, my face still buried.

"I think she might be hungry," Billy offered.

"Hi, Billy," said Mom. "Is everything okay?"

I pulled away and said, "No everything is NOT okay! There's this girl named Emily...and she's really mean...and I didn't do anything to her!" I tried extra hard not to cry.

"That's terrible," my mom said. "What if I have a nice chat with your teacher about her—?"

"No!" I shouted. "Don't do that! Then she'll call me a baby for telling."

"Don't worry, Mrs. Ball," Billy said. "I will be Krystal's personal bodyguard."

"That's thoughtful of you, Billy," Mom said. "But I'm sure we'll figure something out. In the meantime, did anything good happen today?"

"We're putting on a play," Billy answered.

"Really?" asked my mother. "Which one?"

"*The Wizard of Oz*," I said halfheartedly.

"Oh, honey, that's wonderful! You love that story!" Mom exclaimed.

"I know," I said, cracking a smile. Thinking about that book always made me feel better.

"Have you gotten your parts yet?" Mom asked.

"Not yet," Billy said. "I want to be the Tin Woodsman because he gets to hold an axe! How cool is that?" Billy pretended to chop a tree with his hand. "Hi-ya!"

"I want to be Dorothy. She's my favorite," I said. "It's just that...I'm too shy."

"Let me tell you something about the theater," Mom began, placing her hand on my shoulder. "It's a great way to break out of your shell. You can be anyone and anything. People won't be looking at you on that stage—they'll be looking at your character. You have the power to bring that character to life!"

"You're right, Mom," I said. "The truth is...I love Dorothy so much, and I don't want Emily to play her."

Mom chuckled and took my hand. We walked all the way home talking about the play.

***

That night, Mom and Dad kissed me good night. I quickly drifted off to sleep and found myself standing in a long corridor. At the end of the hall was a mirror.

I walked toward my reflection and saw that I was wearing a big, white princess dress that puffed out at the bottom. There were poofy sleeves and sequins all over. Glittering under the light, I walked closer to the mirror.

On top of my head was a crown made of rubies. My curly hair was shining and beautiful.

Wait a minute! I thought.

Suddenly, I realized that the reflection wasn't mine. This wasn't a mirror at all. It was a door. The person standing in front of me had curly black hair and brown eyes.

She smiled and did a curtsy.

"I am Glinda, the Good Witch," she said. Her voice was soft and sweet.

This doesn't look like the Glinda I know from The Wizard of Oz, I thought.

This witch was a young girl, and we were probably the same age.

Glinda took me by the hand and gently pulled me through the doorway.

The light was blinding, and I had to cover my eyes. The sun reflected off a yellow brick road under our feet. On either side of us was a lush forest with tall trees and rainbow-colored flowers.

I heard birds singing happily. They hopped off their perches and fluttered around us before disappearing back into the trees.

"Welcome to Oz," Glinda said. "Follow me, for I have all the answers you seek."

My heart skipped a beat. *How exciting to be in the magical land of Oz!*

As the Good Witch glided away, the yellow brick road started to crumble. It fell away from my feet and into a dark hole below.

I cried out Glinda's name, but she didn't hear me. I struggled to keep up with the Good Witch, but it was too late!

I staggered and fell into darkness.

CHAPTER 3

The Good Witch?

Yellow bricks swirled around me as I tumbled down. Faster and faster I fell. I shut my eyes tight, and then suddenly my body jolted.

I looked around. Pushing a wave of curls out of my face, I realized that I was back in bed. The sun was peeking in through my curtains. My purple star-patterned sheets were a tangled mess at my feet, and my stuffed stegosaurus, Stanley, had fallen off the bed. He was on the floor next to my fuzzy bunny slippers.

I wiped the sleep from my eyes and looked at the clock. I had overslept. Time for school!

Jumping out of bed, I ran straight to the closet. My dream inspired me to wear my yellow leggings and a puffy dress. I topped it off with a warm yellow cardigan. With no time to brush my hair, I swept it up and covered it with one of my

favorite scarves, a red and white polka dot pattern with plastic beads on the trim.

I twirled in the mirror and declared, "Simply fabulous!"

From where he was sitting, Stanley the dinosaur silently agreed.

Suddenly, my ears perked up. I tilted my head and closed my eyes. Another vision!

(Sometimes, I feel that something is going to happen right away. And I'm usually right. Other times, I get mixed signals that I have trouble understanding. Luckily, I'm learning to better control my gift every day.)

As soon as I opened the door, Mom let out a startled gasp. Her hand was raised ready to knock.

"Good morning, Mom!" I said, smiling. "I knew you were there."

Mom smiled back and kissed me on the forehead. "Krystal, it's time for breakfast," she said, walking back down the hall.

I followed her to the kitchen. After I ate my cereal, I went into the hallway to put on my coat and shoes. I closed my eyes and put my hand to my head.

"Billy should be here any second now," I said to my mother.

Then, right on schedule, there was a knock at the door.

"Come in, Billy," I cried.

Billy let himself in. "Good morning, Mrs. Ball," he said. "Hey, Krystal, ready for school?"

"I sure am," I said. "Let's go!"

* * *

Billy's parents, Mr. and Mrs. Katsikis, own a coffee shop around the block from where we live. It's called The House of Sweets. They get up really early to go to work, so my mom and I walk with Billy to school. When we pass by the coffee shop, we always wave Hello.

On our walk, I told Mom and Billy about how Glinda, the Good Witch, was in my dream.

"That could only mean one thing," Billy said. "Miss Callisto is giving out the parts in the school play today. You're going to be Glinda!"

"You really think so?" I asked.

I started to get excited. I forgot about my shyness and imagined Glinda's puffy, glittery white dress and that ruby covered tiara.

"Maybe this play isn't going to be such a disaster after all," I said.

"My darling, no matter what part you get, I'm sure you will be wonderful!" Mom said.

"Thanks, Mom," I replied.

Once we got to the school, Mom kissed me goodbye and left. Billy and I heard the bell ring and bolted up the steps. Inside the classroom, we took our seats and waited for Miss Callisto to scold us for being late. But SHE was missing.

"Where's Miss Callisto?" I whispered to Billy.

"Maybe she took the day off?" he whispered back. "Or maybe she was abducted by aliens!"

"Don't be ridiculous," Emily snapped, overhearing our conversation. "There's no such thing as aliens!"

"Oh, really?" Billy said. "That's EXACTLY what an alien would say! Why don't you call the Mother Ship and have it beam you back home?"

Emily crossed her arms and huffed.

The whispers started getting louder as everyone wondered where Miss Callisto could have gone. Finally the door opened and she walked in.

"Good morning, class. Please settle down." Miss Callisto raised her arms. "My apologies for being late, but I have a special surprise for you."

She waved her hand toward the door, and said, "Everyone, meet our newest student..."

The room fell completely silent as we all held our breaths. A new student was always exciting.

We waited and waited and...nothing happened. Where was the new student?

"Don't be shy, dear. It's all right," Miss Callisto called out to the hallway.

A small girl slowly walked in wearing a red baseball cap with white spots on it. She was looking at the ground so we couldn't see her face.

I liked her outfit, though! She was wearing jeans with flower patches sewn onto them, and her white T-shirt had a sparkling yellow star in the center.

"Class," Miss Callisto announced, "I'm pleased to introduce...Claire Voyance!"

The new girl took off her baseball cap. Rows upon rows of curly black hair tumbled down to her shoulders. I was pleasantly surprised. She had hair just like mine!

Suddenly, my body tingled all over, and I sat pin-straight in my chair. When Claire looked up, I saw that she had a pretty face with brown eyes. I had seen that face before.

Then it hit me.

Before I could stop myself, the words came flying out of my mouth.

"It's Glinda!" I gasped.

CHAPTER 4

New Girl

Everyone turned and stared at me. Slapping my hands over my mouth, I could feel my face burn with embarrassment.

"Krystal, what is the meaning of this outburst?" Miss Callisto asked.

"I'm sorry," I said. "For some reason, Claire reminds me of Glinda, the Good Witch, in *The Wizard of Oz*. Maybe it's the star on her shirt."

My classmates laughed out loud.

Claire smiled at me, and I felt more relaxed. Miss Callisto's face softened, and she smiled, too.

"What a great idea, Krystal!" Then she put her hand on her chin. "Maybe I'll have to reconsider your roles for the play...now that we've found our Glinda! Is that okay with you, Claire?"

"Oh, gosh," she said. "I love *The Wizard of Oz.* I don't know what to say."

Miss Callisto could tell Claire was a little uncomfortable with all the attention, so she changed the subject. "Let's worry about that later," she said. "How about we get you settled in?"

Miss Callisto showed Claire to the empty desk next to mine. I waved at her, and she waved back.

"Welcome," I said. "I didn't mean to shout at you before. It's just that, well, I totally love *The Wizard of Oz,* too."

"Thanks," she said back. "I'm just nervous, but I'm starting to feel better. You're nice, Krystal."

"Thanks," I said. "I really like your hair. And your shirt!"

"I like yours, too!" Claire replied. "And we like the same colors!"

I looked down at my shirt and laughed. "Gosh, you're right!" I said.

Miss Callisto called for our attention and started the lesson. While everyone was working, I kept thinking about my dream. What did it mean?

I had a vision of a complete stranger, and now here she was sitting right next to me!

Then I remembered what happened at the end of the dream, when the yellow brick road crumbled. I shook with fear, so I pushed it to the back of my head until the school day was over.

***

At the end of the day, Billy, Claire, and I were putting on our coats. Emily, Susan, and Kate walked up behind us.

"Hi, Claire," Emily said. "I know you're new here, so we don't want you to make any bad decisions on your first day."

"What do you mean?" Claire asked.

"Oh, like, hanging out with the weirdos like Krystal Ball and Billy Katsikis."

Susan and Kate laughed at Emily's joke.

"Just some friendly advice, new friend," Emily added. "See you tomorrow!"

Susan and Kate laughed again as they walked past. I felt sick to my stomach. Billy grumbled some bad words under his breath.

I couldn't look at Claire so I stared at my shoes. Emily was so annoying I could just scream.

"She's right, you know. I wouldn't want to be seen with weirdos and losers," Claire said. Then she put her hand on my shoulder. "So I am going to stay as far away from those girls as possible!"

I smiled and walked down the steps with Claire and Billy into the schoolyard. Billy saw a group of boys running toward an ice cream truck.

"Excuse me, ladies," Billy said. "But they're playing my song." He rushed past us toward the sound of the ice cream truck's tune. "I'll get a ride home with Joey. See you later!"

Secretly, I was glad that Billy went to play with the boys. It gave me some time alone with Claire. I didn't really have any other close girl friends, and I already felt a special connection to her.

"Hey, Claire, what are you doing after school?" I asked. Before Claire could answer I saw my mom walking up the sidewalk.

"Hey, Mom, over here!" I called out. "This is Claire," I said when she arrived. "She's the new kid in our class."

"Nice to meet you, Claire," Mom said.

"Nice to meet you, too, Mrs. Ball," Claire replied politely.

Moments later, a well-dressed lady walked into the schoolyard. She looked just like Claire, only older. My new friend ran over to her and pulled her by the hand.

"This is Krystal and her mom," she said introducing us.

"A pleasure," Mrs. Voyance responded, extending her hand to shake my mom's.

"How long have you been in Queens?" my mom asked.

"We moved here last week," Mrs. Voyance replied. "We're still getting used to things."

"We've been here as long as I can remember," I said to Mrs. Voyance. "We'd love to show you around if you don't mind. Is that okay, Mom?"

"I've got some free time. We could grab a quick cup of coffee," Mom answered.

"Great," said Mrs. Voyance. "I could sure use one right about now!"

Tugging on my mother's sleeve, I asked, "Can we please go to House of Sweets?" I turned to Claire. "That's the name of the coffee shop that Billy's parents own."

"Wow, cool!" she exclaimed. "He's so lucky!"

"Yup," I agreed. "They've got all sorts of cookies and cakes and treats!"

"Let's go!" she said, smiling from ear to ear.

Soon, the four of us arrived at the bakery. Even from outside, the sweet smell of pastries was strong and inviting. I thought I was floating on a cloud made of sugar and cinnamon.

When we entered the shop, a little bell rang above the door. Mr. and Mrs. Katsikis heard the jingling, looked up, and smiled.

"Please come in, come in, Krystal!" they said together. "How may we help you?"

Our moms greeted Billy's parents and ordered coffees. Claire and I each got a hot chocolate with extra whipped cream. Nothing sweetens up a nasty run-in with Emily like a hot chocolate.

Once we had our drinks, the four of us sat down at a table in front of the cupcake display. There were so many delicious choices.

"What's your favorite cupcake?" I asked Claire.

"Chocolate with peanut butter frosting," she told me.

"Mine too!" I cried. "That's so cool. We're so alike, don't you think?"

"Good friends always are," Claire answered.

Wow! I thought. *A new best friend. Could this day get any sweeter?*

As we sipped our hot chocolates, the whipped cream stuck to our upper lips. We both had white mustaches. At the same time, Claire and I pointed at each other's faces and started giggling. We were having a laughing fit and couldn't stop!

Suddenly, my body tingled. I was getting a vision. I closed my eyes and tilted my head.

I heard Claire ask, "Krystal, are you okay?"

I held up my hand as the vision came into focus. Several shards of broken glass were falling and swirling around something gooey and sticky. My ears perked up, and I opened my eyes.

At the other end of the store, I saw Mr. Katsikis carrying a heavy tray full of dishes and glasses. He was heading toward the kitchen door.

"Mr. K., LOOK OUT!" I cried.

Billy's dad stopped in his tracks. He turned and looked at me with a puzzled expression. Just then, the kitchen door banged open as one of the bakers came out carrying a tall layer cake.

I gasped. If Mr. Katsikis had kept walking, he would have crashed into the baker. The dishes, glasses, and cake would have splattered everywhere.

"Thank you, Krystal," Mr. K. said and continued on his way. We both looked relieved.

Turning back toward Claire, I noticed she was staring at me. Her mouth was slightly opened, and the mug of hot chocolate never made its way to her lips.

She put the mug down slowly. Finally she spoke. "How...how did you do that?" she asked.

"Do what?" I said. I took a sip of my cocoa and felt my face get hot again. I pretended everything was fine.

"It's like you knew something bad was going to happen and you stopped it."

"I'm not Supergirl," I said, letting out a nervous laugh.

"That's not what I meant," Claire said, shaking her head. "More like you had a sixth sense. Like you're psychic or something!"

"What? NO!" I said, raising my voice.

My hands shook, and I placed the cup of cocoa on the table so I wouldn't spill it. No one, aside from my family and Billy, knew about my gifts. Most people weren't as observant as Claire.

I was confused. Deep down I wanted to let her in on my big secret. She was my new best friend, after all.

I didn't know what to do.

"Krystal, what's wrong?" Claire asked.

A loud group of teenage girls walked in carrying dozens of shopping bags. Chattering away on their cell phones, they sat at the table next to us. It was too loud to talk, and we didn't have any privacy.

I leaned in close to Claire and said, "I better not tell you now."

CHAPTER 5

A Twister

That night, I dreamed of Oz again. It must have been on my mind.

In my dream, I was home alone in our apartment. Winds howled through window cracks and tree branches scraped against the pane. I pulled back my curtain slightly to peek outside. The sky was gray and everything looked gloomy. A mighty gust of wind ripped a branch off the tree. It hit the trunk and snapped in half.

CRAAACK!

I yelped and ran under the covers.

Suddenly, the room rumbled. The walls shook. The dresser rattled. My porcelain dolls teetered on their stands until they tumbled to the floor.

Soon, the entire building pitched forward and backward until it lurched...upward! I tried to keep my balance as the floor under me spun around in circles. Looking out the window again, I was shocked at the sight. And what a sight it was!

The building was swirling and whirling inside the center of a cyclone. It flew faster and faster. It went high up over Queens, over the city, and continued over farmlands. In the distance, through the downpour and thunderclouds, I thought I saw a rainbow.

Just as quickly, the building started to come down. I sprinted to the bed and under the covers once again. Hugging Stanley close to my chest, I shut my eyes and held my breath.

THUD!

The building landed hard. I peeked my head out and thought, *What a mess!* If my mother were here she'd say that my room looked like a tornado passed through it. In this case, she'd be right!

Cradling Stanley in my arm, I brushed the curls out of my face and opened my bedroom door. Instead of the hallway of my home, I found myself in the town square of a tiny village.

The cottages were a little taller than I was, and each painted a bright pastel color. Our crumbling, lopsided apartment building stood out like a giant weed in a pretty garden.

"Whoa," I said to Stanley. "Something tells me we're not in Queens anymore."

An object shimmering in the sun caught my attention. It was near the far corner of my busted building. Together, Stanley and I investigated.

That was when I saw them. There, sticking out from some broken wood and a pile of bricks, was a pair of legs! Human legs clad in long black stockings! Each foot had on a beautiful, shiny, silver slipper that reflected the sunlight.

I was shocked and horrified. I didn't know what I had done or what to do.

And so, I screamed.

CHAPTER 6

Wicked Witch?

The next day at school, I had a headache and felt groggy. The rest of the class was buzzing with excitement. Miss Callisto announced that she was handing out our roles for *The Wizard of Oz*.

I had an uneasy feeling in my stomach that lingered from my dream. Just to be extra careful, I wore my crystal necklace and charm bracelets. Crystals are supposed to have magical properties, and the charm bracelet was for good luck. I needed all the luck I could get!

"Okay, everybody!" Miss Callisto said, clapping her hands.

The class fell silent. She walked to the center of the room holding a stack of scripts.

"Let's start with the title role of the Great and Powerful Wizard of Oz himself!" she announced. "Billy Katsikis!"

Billy bowed dramatically. "I am Billy, the great and powerful!" he bellowed. Everyone laughed.

"And now," Miss Callisto continued, "onto our witches. First up is Glinda, the Good Witch. Let's hear it for...Claire Voyance!"

Our classmates applauded as Claire walked up to the teacher. My body started to tingle. Something was about to happen. I knew it. I clutched the crystal at my chest. Whatever it was, it was coming soon.

Miss Callisto spoke again. "The other witch in our play," she said, "is the Wicked Witch of the West. She will be played by...Krystal Ball!"

Oh no! I wanted to crawl under the desk and disappear.

I looked at Claire. She tried to smile, but I'm sure she knew how I felt. No one wants to be the Wicked Witch of the West, right?

I looked over at Billy. He was smiling from ear to ear. He gave me a thumbs up. "You're so lucky," he said. "The bad guys are the best!"

Miss Callisto called me to the front of the room. Dragging my feet, I walked over and picked up my script. Then she continued giving out roles, but I didn't hear a word she said. I stared at the sheets of paper in front of me. There it was in big, bold letters: WICKED WITCH OF THE WEST: KRYSTAL BALL.

"My favorite part is when the witch melts," Billy said. He snatched the script off my desk. "Do you want to practice together? I can show you how to make the death scene look real."

Billy clutched his throat. "I'm dying," he gasped and made gurgling, gagging sounds.

"I'm dying," he said again and rolled his eyes back into his head. Kicking his legs out in front of him, he slid down off his chair onto the floor.

He stuck his tongue out and said, "I'm dead!"

The kids laughed until the teacher told him to stop.

"And last but not least," Miss Callisto continued, "we have the role of Dorothy Gale."

My ears perked up, and I closed my eyes. "Oh no," I whispered. "Outlook not so good…"

"Emily Heart!" Miss Callisto declared.

The students clapped, except for me and Billy.

"Oh thank you, thank you!" Emily said. She fake-smiled and waved at us like a beauty pageant queen. "I always knew I was born to be a star!"

As she walked past me to get her script, something caught my attention. I looked down and saw what it was.

Suddenly, my skin started to prickle like hundreds of tiny little bugs were crawling on it.

Emily was wearing long black stockings and a pair of shiny, silver slippers. Just like the ones in my dream sticking out from under my house!

Holding her head high, Emily walked back to her desk. Her shiny hair bounced behind her.

She looked down her nose at me and said, "I need to get into character. That's what real actors do. So I'm going to treat you like my enemy!"

Susan and Kate leaned out of their seats to congratulate Emily. They were so happy for her. Susan got the part of Aunt Em and Kate was playing a Munchkin.

I was so jealous. I would've traded parts with either of them. I just didn't want to be the Wicked Witch and an even bigger target for Emily's meanness.

And that was just it! Emily was the mean one. SHE should be the wicked witch. Not me!

Billy saw my troubled face and asked, "Hey Krystal, what's the matter?"

"A little less noise, please," Miss Callisto called from her desk.

I tore a piece of paper out of my notebook and quickly scribbled the message: "Emily wearing same outfit as my dream. Must be a vision of what is going to happen in the future."

Folding the piece of paper into a little triangle, I passed it to Billy when the teacher wasn't looking.

He opened it, read it, and wrote something underneath my message. Then he passed it me.

I opened it and read: "Is it bad?"

Closing my eyes and tilting my head, I tried to focus on the vision from my dream. A new sensation passed through my body, and I was certain.

Writing my answer down, I passed the paper back to Billy. He opened it up:

CHAPTER 7

Dress Rehearsal

A couple weeks passed. Our class was focused on putting on the best fourth-grade play anyone had ever seen in the history of Nikola Tesla Elementary School.

During this time, Emily made everyone's lives particularly miserable. Not just mine. This "star of the show" attitude that she had was getting old. Emily was bossy and would throw a fit if she was not the center of attention. She even managed to push away her best friends, Susan and Kate.

Even so, I was actually enjoying myself. When I put on my costume, with its pointy black hat and long black dress, I felt like another person. I wasn't Krystal Ball, fourth-grade fortune-teller. I was Krystal Ball, Wicked Witch!

Claire looked beautiful in her puffy, sparkling white gown and ruby-crusted crown. "We are mirror images of each other," Claire pointed out.

"You're right!" I said with a laugh.

We giggled again as Billy came up behind us. He was wearing a green suit and vest, with a glittering green blazer over them. His usually messy hair had been slicked back and looked very dashing. "Behold, the Great and Powerful—"

Miss Callisto clapped her hands, interrupting Billy. She told us to form a line.

"Listen up, class," she said. "We're going to the auditorium for our dress rehearsal. We'll be performing on stage as if it was the real night of the play."

How exciting is that? I thought to myself. *This is going to be so much fun.*

For someone who could see the future, I could not have been more wrong...

"Okay, everyone, let's take it from the top of the scene!" Miss Callisto cried from the back of the auditorium.

We were up to the part where the Wicked Witch of the West (me) captures Dorothy (the annoying Emily) and friends in her giant castle. The Witch wants to take Dorothy's Silver Shoes because they are full of magic and power.

Dorothy then throws a bucket of water onto the Wicked Witch, causing her to melt away.

Instead of real water, Miss Callisto filled a plastic bucket with blue, green, and white confetti and glitter. When Emily splashed the fake water onto me, I would spin around and drop onto the ground. Then, I'd pull my black cloak over myself and lie still until the curtains closed.

And so, we began.

"Give me the Silver Shoes," I cried in my witchiest voice.

"You are a wicked creature," Emily said while reaching for the bucket.

A split-second later, the bucket came sailing through the air right at me. I dodged it, but it grazed off my shoulder. It really hurt, too! I rubbed my arm as the bucket landed behind me.

"Krystal, are you all right?" Claire asked, running out from behind the scenery.

"Yeah," I said, looking at Emily. She didn't seem the least bit sorry. She did it on purpose!

Miss Callisto walked onto the stage. "Oh my goodness!" she exclaimed.

"Clumsy me," Emily said. She clasped her hands dramatically. "Accidents happen." Emily reached over and put her hand on my shoulder. "You poor thing!"

I flinched and then something happened. I caught a glimpse of the future.

I closed my eyes and tilted my head. Emily's touch sparked a memory. My dream about the tornado and my house landing on someone came flooding back in an instant.

Without opening my eyes, and in a low whisper, I said, "Yes...accidents *do* happen."

BRIIIING! The bell rang. It was time for lunch. I couldn't wait to change and put the whole nasty event behind me.

As Billy and I sat at our lunch table, I asked, "Remember when I said something bad was going to happen to Emily?"

"Yeah," he said, smiling widely. Peanut butter and jelly was stuck to his teeth. "I keep waiting for this dream to come true!"

"That's not funny," I said, but Billy's face made me laugh. "I got a strong feeling when she touched me. It was just like the day she broke my pencil. Something's going to happen today. I don't know what it is or what to do."

"There's nothing to do," Billy said. "She's a nasty person, and she deserves whatever she gets. Are you gonna eat that?" Billy reached over and snagged one of my carrot sticks.

I wanted to believe Billy. What he said sounded right, but the knot in my stomach told me otherwise.

"What would you tell her, anyway?" Billy continued. Bits of carrot sloshed around in his mouth. "Beware, Emily! My psychic powers tell me that something bad is going to happen to you, so don't do anything for it may be your doom!"

Before I could reply, a voice cried out behind us. "I knew it!"

I whirled around to see…Claire. She had been standing nearby holding her lunch box. Her eyes were as wide as saucers.

My body went numb. Billy's mouth dropped open. The carrot stick landed on his lunch tray.

"Oops," he said weakly.

"H-how much did you hear?" I stammered.

Claire placed her lunch box on the table and sat down next to me. Looking me in the eye, she said, "Everything!"

CHAPTER 8

Break a Leg

During recess, kids ran hollering onto the playground. Billy, Claire, and I were the last ones out. Once we were alone, Claire pulled us behind a tall tree at the corner of the schoolyard.

She put her hands on her hips. "Okay, Ball, spill it!" Claire said. Then she pointed her finger at me. "I knew there was something special about you the first time we met. I guess you could say I have a sixth sense about these things, too."

Billy and I traded looks. He shifted uncomfortably. I sighed and took a deep breath.

"Look, Claire, this is serious stuff," I said. "If I tell you the truth, you have to promise not to say anything. Ever."

Claire got excited. She hopped up and down and said, "Krystal, that's what best friends do. They trust each other, and they help each other."

Hearing this made me feel better. I wanted another friend to understand me the same way Billy does. And so, I decided to share my secret with Claire.

"Here goes…" I said.

I told my new best friend everything about my gift: my extra abilities, the dreams, the visions, and the feelings and sensations. I even told Claire about my grandma.

"My grandma has the same gift as me," I said. "And sometimes, when I need guidance, I ask her what to do. She's so wise and knows so much about everything!"

Claire stood there staring at Billy and me. Her eyes were bugging out, and her mouth was wide open. It seemed like forever.

"Claire, say something," I begged. "You're starting to freak me out."

"Yeah," Billy added. "You look like my goldfish, Leonidas."

Claire inhaled and exhaled slowly.

"Whoa…" she finally said. "Ohmygosh!" She reached out and hugged me. "You're the coolest person I ever met! Your secret is safe, bestie!"

"So now you know," Billy said. "Welcome to the club."

He took a step toward Claire and said in his best gangster voice, "If you tell a soul, you'll be sleeping with my fishes."

"Billy, stop that!" I told him. Then to Claire, "Do you pinkie-promise you won't say anything?"

"Of course I do," she said.

We linked pinkies, forming the sacred bond of the pinkie promise.

Meanwhile, over on the playground, another momentous event was about to take place.

Emily had climbed up to the top of the jungle gym. She was still wearing her Dorothy costume.

"I am Dorothy, the Queen of Oz," she shouted at the top of her lungs. Her perfect pigtails and blue gingham dress fluttered in the breeze. "And you are all my loyal subjects."

Emily stood up on the highest metal rung. The other kids stopped and watched.

"Bow down to your queen," Emily hollered.

"I don't remember this part in the book," I said to Billy and Claire. We ran over to the jungle gym.

Looking up, I noticed that Emily's silver shoes had smooth, shiny soles. They were not the best things to wear when standing on a metal bar.

"Emily, I don't think that's safe," I shouted.

"If it isn't the Wicked Witch herself. Look, everybody," Emily said with a laugh. "She's trying to steal my wonderful shoes!"

Everyone turned to look at me. They started laughing too. I felt my cheeks burning hot. I closed my eyes and took a deep breath, like Grandma taught me. I focused my mind toward the wind rustling through the trees.

The wind blew harder. It whistled through the branches...just like the tornado in my dream. My skin tingled, and my eyes snapped open.

"Look at me. I'm a star!" Emily shouted. She waved her arms up and down.

Suddenly, a powerful gust of wind blew through the playground. Emily lost her balance and screamed. Her silver shoes slipped on the rung and sent her plummeting off the jungle gym.

CRAAACK!

When Emily hit the ground, it sounded like a pencil snapping.

The kids gasped and made way as the playground monitor ran over. "Are you all right, dear?" she asked.

"My ankle!" Emily shrieked. "Is it broken?"

The monitor carried Emily inside. We could hear her sobs echo down the hallway.

Billy turned to us and said, "Yup. She's a star all right. A falling star!" He laughed at his joke.

Claire and I exchanged worried looks. "You were right," Claire said. "You saw the future. Do you know what's going to happen next?"

I closed my eyes and tried to concentrate.

It was no use.

I turned toward Claire and said, "Reply hazy. Ask again later…"

CHAPTER 9

Accessorize!

Later that afternoon, Billy and Claire came over to my house. We were sitting in my bedroom discussing Emily's accident.

"The school nurse says that Emily sprained her ankle. It's swollen and she needs to wear an air cast over it." Claire said. "Then her dad came and picked her up."

"Good riddance," Billy replied. "I hope they went back to her home planet."

"This is no time for jokes, Billy," I reminded him. "The nurse says that Emily can walk in the cast by the play's opening night. That makes me feel hopeful."

"But did you hear what happened after?" Claire asked. "Susan and Kate said that Emily's foot was so swollen and ugly it couldn't fit into her silver shoe. She told them that there was no way she would play Dorothy wearing her air cast and to forget the whole show!"

"But isn't it a famous saying that the show must go on?" said Billy.

"Without a Dorothy!?" I exclaimed. "There is no show!"

"Bah," Billy said waving his arm. "Paint a smiley-face on a pumpkin, slap it on a broomstick, throw a wig on it, and call it Dorothy. No one will even notice."

Claire and I chuckled.

"It'll be more pleasant than the real Emily, that's for sure." I said. "Now let's get serious. There's only one thing to do in a crisis like this. Consult the cards!"

I got up and walked to my dresser. Picking up a small, hand-carved wooden box, I opened it and pulled out the tarot cards Grandma gave me on my birthday.

"The tarot cards will provide guidance. They always show the right path to the future," I said fanning them out face down on the carpet.

Then I reached under my bed to pull out a thick leather-bound book. This helped me understand how the cards could be interpreted. (Another gift from Grandma. Isn't she the best?)

Billy and Claire leaned in closer. They held their breath as I picked up the first card.

It had an image of a beautiful woman seated on a throne. She had on a long white dress and a light blue cape that draped around her feet. On her head was a light blue and white crown. There was a column on each side of the throne. One black, and the other white.

I read the name of the card, "The High Priestess."

Leafing through the leather-bound book I found the chapter on the High Priestess and read aloud: "The High Priestess symbolizes Knowingness, Love, Wisdom, Intuition, and Mystical Vision. She is an interpreter of secrets and mystery and is one who holds onto the truth or reveals it. Commonly this card is associated with the card reader."

We silently exchanged looks as I picked up another card. "The Chariot."

A powerful, princely figure wearing a golden crown was sitting in a chariot being pulled by two sphinxes. One was black and the other was white.

"Ooh, can I?" Claire asked, pointing to the book.

"Sure," I said.

Claire started reading. "The Chariot is one of the most complex cards to define. On its most basic level, it implies a struggle and an eventual hard-won victory over an enemy or obstacle. Qualities needed to win the battle include self-reliance, discipline, bravery, and pride."

Then she continued, "The steeds represent powerful forces that can be controlled to achieve the goal. Because they are opposites, it is the Charioteer's duty to use willpower and conviction to unite them."

"Whoa, that's some heavy stuff," Billy said.

I sat quietly trying to take it all in.

Then I turned over the final card. "The Magician," I told them.

The picture showed a man wearing a long red robe cinched in the middle by a golden belt. His arm was raised over his head and in his hand he held a magic wand.

I pulled the book back toward me and started reading.

"The characteristics defined by the Magician are Concentration, Personal Power, Creativity, Self-Confidence, and Initiative. When the Magician appears in a spread, it points to the talents, capabilities, and resources at one's disposal. There are choices and directions to take. Guidance can arrive through one's own intuition or in the form of those who bring about change or transformation around them."

I closed my eyes. Images from the cards floated around in my head. I thought my brain was going to burst.

Finally, I made a decision.

I sighed and said, "We have to help Emily."

"Yes," Claire agreed. "You're right. It's the only way to save the play."

Billy stood up and cried, "Is this real life? Has the planet gone mad?"

He put his hands on his head, "Why should we be nice to that brat after all she put us through? Let her suffer!"

"Billy, the point is that we're all in this together. If Emily doesn't participate, all the hard work we put into this project will be lost," Claire explained.

"Who cares? So we don't have to put on our silly costumes and waste our time on a Saturday," Billy huffed. "I'd rather sit at home, watch cartoons, and eat pizza!"

"Now you're just being stubborn and selfish," Claire shot back.

"Me? Stubborn?" Billy shouted. "I'll show you stubborn!" Billy crossed his arms and turned his back.

"Fine!" Claire shouted back and did the same.

I stood there as my best friends fumed.

Suddenly, it was all clear. I had a choice to make, a path to take, and two stubborn steeds to unite.

If I could do all that, then I would really be Krystal Ball, the Great and Powerful!

"ENOUGH!" I shouted, jolting Claire and Billy out of their feud.

They looked at me with eyes open wide. They may have even been a little frightened.

"Now that I have your attention, here's my plan," I said. "First, we're going to apologize to each other and work together. Like Claire said, best friends need to trust each other. We also need to be united for this to work."

"Well, she started it," Billy complained.

"I don't want to hear it," I said putting up my hand. I felt just like my mother. "You're both being stubborn donkeys."

Claire giggled. "Donkey is such a funny word."

I smiled.

Billy said, "My grandpa has a pet donkey in Greece. He's really stubborn, and he's named after my father!"

Claire and I started laughing.

"I'm sorry I called you stubborn," Claire quietly said to Billy.

"That's okay," Billy replied. "The truth is, I am! Are we friends again?"

"Of course. Best friends!" Claire said and shook his hand.

"Excellent," I told them. "Now, here's what we're going to do..."

I walked over to my desk. "In order for the show to go on," I said, "we're going to help Emily back on her feet and into those Silver Shoes."

"But remember how her foot looks like an eggplant now?" Billy said.

Claire laughed again. "He's right. And besides, why would she want help from us? We're her *enemies*," Claire said, making quotation marks with her fingers.

"Yes, but remember the tarot cards?" I asked. "They represented each one of us. Claire is the High Priestess, Billy is the Magician, and I am the Charioteer. We need to combine our special talents to overcome this obstacle."

"All right, Chief Charioteer," Billy said with a salute. "What did you have in mind?"

"Glad you asked." I reached into my desk. Inside were bins full of arts and crafts supplies.

Lifting it out, I said, "We are going to improvise and accessorize!"

"That sounds like an exciting adventure to me," said Claire, placing an arm around Billy and myself.

"The Wizard, the Witches, and the Wardrobe!" I exclaimed.

CHAPTER 10

On With the Show

The next day at school, Emily hobbled in wearing the air cast on her swollen ankle. She looked more cranky than usual.

"Good morning, Emily. How do you feel today?" Miss Callisto asked.

"Miserable," she responded. "I'm not doing the play. My air cast is ugly, and I look stupid!"

The class gasped in unison. They all looked disappointed.

It was time to put our plan into action.

"Miss Callisto," I said, raising my hand. "Billy, Claire, and I have a solution to the problem."

Emily glared at me. "Are you saying I'm the problem?"

Instead of getting defensive, I smiled sweetly. "I know you're worried about your foot and the cast," I explained. "So we thought we would help you out."

Emily eyed us suspiciously as I carried over my arts and crafts bin.

"What are you going to do?" Miss Callisto asked, puzzled.

The class huddled around.

"You'll see," I answered. "Will you let us help you, Emily? I promise we only want what's best for you and the whole class."

Emily looked at us, then around the room, and back at us again. "I...guess," she replied.

First, I placed a large sheet of newspaper on Emily's desk.

"Put your swollen foot on the desk," Billy said.

Emily shot him an angry look but did as he said.

"Trust me," Billy added. "I'm a wizard!"

He pulled out my glue bottle from the bin. Billy uncapped the lid and dipped a paintbrush in it. Smiling widely, Billy smeared the air cast from top to bottom with gobs of white glue. It looked all sticky and slimy.

"Eww, gross!" Emily cried.

Billy capped the glue and wiped the brush with a paper towel.

"NEXT!" he cried.

Claire and I stood on either side of Emily's foot. Billy passed us a small container. In it, were silver beads, sequins, rhinestones, and fake diamonds that I got at a costume and magic shop.

The two of us started to apply the accessories onto the air cast. In a couple minutes, her footwear was unrecognizable. Studded with jewels, it looked more like Dorothy's Silver Shoe than an air cast.

"But wait, there's more!" Billy cried, pulling out a spray can and a bottle of glitter.

"And now for the finishing touches," I said.

Claire sprayed the cast with aerosol adhesive. Then I sprinkled glitter all over our work of art. It sparkled and shimmered in the light as if it were made of magic.

Everyone in the class oohed and aahed.

"Ta-da!" I said holding up my arms.

Miss Callisto smiled and started clapping. The rest of the class followed.

"BRAVO, children!" she said to me, Billy, and Claire. "What an excellent and creative idea!"

Emily's frown turned upside down.

"WOW!" She exclaimed, admiring our

handiwork. She stood and showed off her new footwear. "I can't believe it! It's so cool. You guys—"

Then Emily caught herself and stopped. She bit her lower lip and looked at the floor.

"You guys are really nice," she whispered.

Then she looked up at me with big sad eyes. "I'm really sorry for the way I treated you, Krystal," Emily said. "I should not have been so mean. Only a real friend would do such a nice thing. Will you be my friend?"

I was surprised by Emily's sudden change. All the bad energy between us washed away.

"Thank you for apologizing, Emily," I said. "You did hurt my feelings a lot…but I forgive you. Of course I will be your friend!"

Emily gave me a hug.

"I think we can all learn a lesson from Krystal," Miss Callisto said to the class. "A small act of kindness can make a big difference! Now, we have one last rehearsal before the big night tomorrow."

"Let's get this show on the road," Emily said. "We are all going to be stars!"

"And as they say in show business," I replied, "break a leg!"

The whole class laughed at my joke, but Emily laughed the hardest.

* * *

Finally, it was the night of the play. All our preparation and hard work was about to pay off. Miss Callisto's fourth grade class was in costume and standing behind the scenes.

My unruly curls were wrapped up in my lucky green scarf and piled high atop my head. That way my pointy black hat could stay on without falling off. I was wearing a floor-length black costume dress with long sleeves. Tied around my neck was a sheer black cloak that dragged on the floor behind me.

I knew I was supposed to be ugly and evil, but I felt so fabulous!

I peeked around the curtain and saw that the auditorium was packed. Every student at Nikola Tesla Elementary School was there and they had brought their friends and families. What a turnout!

Nervously, I twisted the cape in my hands. There were butterflies in my stomach and I wished they would fly away.

I closed my eyes and tried to see the future, but suddenly Miss Callisto whispered, "It's show time!"

And before I knew it, the rest of the night was a blur.

There were some very memorable moments.

First, Claire looked fabulous as Glinda. Her curly black hair and puffy white sequined gown shined under the spotlight. The rubies on her tiara twinkled like Christmas tree lights.

Billy looked dashing in his green suit as the Wizard of Oz.

When he yelled, "I am OZ the GREAT and POWERFUL!" his voiced boomed out over the crowd. It even frightened a few of the younger children.

Also, when Emily made her entrance as Dorothy, there was a loud round of applause. She even got some laughs because the audience thought her sparkly, silver air cast was cute and funny.

Smiling proudly, Emily turned to show off all the shimmering stones and glitter. She really did look like a star after all!

The greatest highlight of the night was my big moment at the end of the play. It was the moment when Dorothy defeats the Wicked Witch of the West and saves her friends.

Emily and I exchanged our lines and Emily reached for the bucket. Inside was an even bigger batch of blue glitter and confetti.

"You wicked creature!" Emily cried. "You have no right to take my shoes from me."

She splashed me with the glittering mixture.

WHOOSH!

"See what you have done," I screamed. "In a minute, I shall melt away!"

And with that, I grabbed my cape and whirled and twirled in a circle near the edge of the stage.

The glitter and confetti lifted off my dress like a sparkling rain shower. It sprinkled the people sitting the front row. They all cheered with delight.

Quickly, I dropped to the ground, laying flat on my back, and pulled the cloak over my head.

Through the fabric of the cloak, I could see the audience jump to their feet. They started clapping wildly. I had gotten a standing ovation! I couldn't believe it.

How wonderful, I thought. *They like me. They really like me!*

Then the curtain fell and I got back on my feet. Before I knew it, my classmates had surrounded me. Everyone was cheering, and high-fiving, and hugging each other.

"You did it!" Miss Callisto shouted over the applause. "Bravo!!"

A few minutes later, our parents came backstage to greet us. Mom and Dad brought me a big bouquet of roses. They smelled lovely.

"Congratulations, sweetheart," Mom said.

"I knew you could do it," Dad added.

My heart swelled with joy. "Thank you," I said.

Billy, Claire, and Emily came over to my family. We congratulated each other on our great performances.

Emily said, "We are the biggest hit to ever happen at our school!"

"Are you sure?" Billy asked. "Your performance on the playground was a pretty big hit, too!"

Emily playfully elbowed Billy and said, "Yes it was. And I hope there's never an encore."

"Thanks to you," Claire said putting her arm around me, "we saved the play and saved the day!"

Billy added, "Let's hear it for Krystal Ball. She knows all and sees all!"

Emily, Claire, and Billy cheered. My cheeks felt hot and I blushed. Usually I'm very shy and quiet and don't want to be the center of attention.

But this time, I earned it.

Puffing out my chest, I linked arms with my three friends. "I am Krystal Ball...the Great and Powerful!" I said, laughing. "With a little help from my friends, of course."

Ruby Ann Phillips

Ruby Ann Phillips is the pseudonym of a *New York Times* bestselling author who lives in the Big Apple, in a neighborhood much like Krystal Ball's.

Sernur Isik

Sernur Isik lives in magical Istanbul, Turkey. As a child, she loved drawing fairies and unicorns, as well as wonderful, imaginative scenes of her home country. Since graduating from the Fine Arts Faculty-Graphic Design of Ataturk University, Sernur has worked as a professional illustrator and artist for children's books, mascot designs, and textile brands.

Glossary

ABDUCTED (ab-DUHKT-id)—taken away by force

ACCESSORIZE (ak-SES-ur-ize)—to wear or decorate with accessories

AEROSOL (AIR-uh-sawl)—a product, such as deodorant or insecticide, that is sold in a spray can

ASTROLOGY (as-TRAH-luh-jee)—the study of the how the positions of stars affect humans

CONVICTION (kuhn-VIK-shuhn)—a strong belief or opinion

DISCIPLINE (DIS-uh-plin)—control over your own or someone else's behavior

INITIATIVE (i-NISH-uh-tiv)—the ability to take action without being told what to do

MEDIUM (MEE-dee-uhm)—a person who claims to communicate with the spirits of dead people

Horoscopes by Krystal Ball!

Astrologists believe a diagram of the position of stars and planets on a person's birthday fortells the future. This diagram is divided into twelve groups called signs. Find your sign and Krystal's prediction for your future!

ARIES (MAR 21–APR 19)

Krystal says: "You love helping others. Soon, someone will need your help. But they might not always ask, so make sure to offer your helping hand!"
Lucky numbers: 9, 15, 33

TAURUS (APR 20–MAY 20)

Krystal says: "The outdoors are calling you lately! Pack a lunch and hit the trail, or take out a magnifying glass and get to know some bugs."
Lucky numbers: 2, 18, 49

GEMINI (MAY 21–JUN 21)

Krystal says: "Your family and friends know you love them, but it's nice to be reminded once in a while! Make them something to show you care."
Lucky numbers: 1, 24, 91

CANCER (JUN 22–JUL 22)

Krystal says: "Have you been bored lately, Cancer? Try out a new hobby and then share it with a friend!"
Lucky numbers: 6, 21, 75

LEO (JUL 23–AUG 22)

Krystal says: "Leo, you've been feeling creative these days. Channel your creativity into a cool project, like building a bird house or writing a story."
Lucky numbers: 12, 53, 67

VIRGO (AUG 23–SEP 22)

Krystal says: "Have you been feeling rushed lately by others around you? Take a second to relax and figure out exactly what YOU need."
Lucky numbers: 14, 36, 42

LIBRA (SEP 23–OCT 22)

Krystal says: "There's a great opportunity coming your way, Libra. Get ready to run with it, whatever it is!"
Lucky numbers: 4, 27, 83

SCORPIO (OCT 23–NOV 21)

Krystal says: "You are always on the go, go, go! Take an hour or two and spend some time in peace and quiet."
Lucky numbers: 3, 31, 62

SAGITTARIUS (NOV 22–DEC 21)

Krystal says: "Your smile is a strength, Sagittarius. You never know what will happen when you flash those pearly whites!"
Lucky numbers: 19, 25, 64

CAPRICORN (DEC 22–JAN 19)

Krystal says: "Feeling chatty lately? Be sure to get out there and make some new friends!"
Lucky numbers: 15, 37, 80

AQUARIUS (JAN 20–FEB 18)

Krystal says: "You're way ahead of the trends, Aquarius. Pick just one to master, whether it's fashion, art, music, or sports."
Lucky numbers: 7, 38, 95

PISCES (FEB 19–MAR 20)

Krystal says: "You give great advice, Pisces, but sometimes all a friend needs is a listening ear, so sit back and take it in!"
Lucky numbers: 20, 41, 73

Krystal's Fortune Game!

What you'll need:
- Markers, crayons, or colored pencils
- A square piece of paper
- One or more friends!

1. First, fold your square piece of paper diagonally in half to make a triangle. Make sure there is a crease. Then, open it up again.

2. Fold the paper diagonally the opposite way to make a second triangle. When you open the paper up again, there should be two creases in the shape of an X.

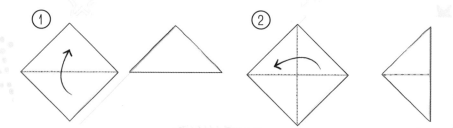

3. Next, take one corner of your paper and fold it toward the center. Repeat with each corner of the square. All the corners should meet in the center of the square.

4. Flip over the paper so that the folded side is face down.

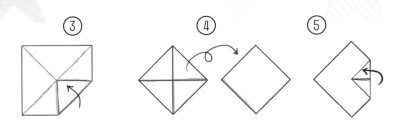

5. Repeat steps 3 and 4 to make a smaller square.

6. Keep the fortune teller folded side up and write the numbers 1-8 in each of the creased triangles. There should be only one number in each triangle.

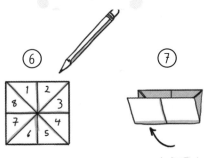

7. Open each flap and write a fortune on the inside of each triangle. You should have two fortunes written inside each flap.

8. Close the flaps back up, and flip the fortune teller over. Now color each of the four squares a different color. Once you've colored them in, you're ready to predict the future!

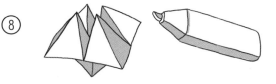

See what the future holds for...

Krystal Ball

Read another book to find out!

Krystal Ball

DREAM BIRTHDAY
by Ruby Ann Phillips

THE FUN DOESN'T STOP HERE!

Discover more at www.capstonekids.com

Videos & Contests/Games & Puzzles
Friends & Favorites/Authors & Illustrators

Find cool websites and more books like this one at www.facthound.com.
Just type in the Book ID: 9781479521791 and you are ready to go!